Super Special #5

The Case of the Four-Leaf Clover

Read all the Jigsaw Jones Mysteries!

And Don't Miss . . .

To my grandma. And to Craig Walker, who loved a good story.

— M.B.

With a nod of appreciation to Alfred Hitchcock's classic film Rear Window.

ISBN-13: 978-0-545-03837-9
ISBN-10: 0-545-03837-5

Text copyright © 2008 by James Preller
Illustrations copyright © 2008 by Scholastic Inc.

12 11 10 9 8 7 6 5 4 3 2 1   8 9 10 11 12 13/0

Printed in the U.S.A.
First printing, March 2008

Super Special #5

The Case of the
Four-Leaf Clover

written by Maria Barbo
based on the characters
created by James Preller

illustrated by Jamie Smith
cover illustration by R. W. Alley

SCHOLASTIC INC.
New York Toronto London Auckland Sydney
Mexico City New Delhi Hong Kong Buenos Aires

CONTENTS

Chapter One

Ouch!

It was just another ho-hum Wednesday afternoon. Except that there was nothing "hum" or "ho" about it.

I sat in front of my bedroom window and watched the world go by. And it did — like a snail on crutches.

My foot was propped up on a stack of old jigsaw puzzles. And my ankle felt more banged up than a tin drum. I had sprained it two days ago, playing baseball. Too bad Bigs Maloney mistook it for a game of "kill the man with the ball." Bigs slid hard into

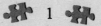

second base. I know, because I happened to be standing on second base at the time. The big lug plowed into me like I was a pile of snow. I have one word for when that happens.

Ouch.

Now I had to give my ankle plenty of rest. That meant no school until next week. It was great for about an hour and a half. After that, it got old real fast.

By Wednesday, I'd already spent two full days sitting around with nothing to do but stare out the window. Sure, it was a nice enough window. But to me it was just a pane. If I didn't get back to solving mysteries, I was going to do something drastic. Like homework.

See, I'm a detective. For a dollar a day, I make problems go away. And a detective without a case is like an ice-cream sundae without the hot fudge. Why bother?

 2

So I stared out my window into the backyard and hoped that something mysterious would suddenly appear.

As luck would have it, it did.

Go figure.

Chapter Two
Trouble

I rolled over to my closet and fished out a pair of binoculars. See, I'd been spending my time on a chair with wheels. I had crutches, too, but they hurt my armpits.

Nobody likes achy armpits.

I scooted back to the window ledge and peered through the binoculars.

Four-year-old Sally Ann Simms was in her yard, next to mine. She wore a lavender tutu and danced around like some kind of crazy ballerina hopped up on Froot Loops and Sugar Bombz. Yeesh.

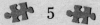

Nothing too mysterious there.

Suddenly, I heard a *thump* and a *crash*! The sounds came from outside the house next door. My neighbor Wingnut O'Brien had just banged into a bunch of garbage cans. It seemed he

was pretending that his hamster, Hermie, could fly like Superman. But that's not the weird part. Wingnut had the poor little rodent dressed up in a red cape.

Clearly, I was surrounded by loony tunes.

I tilted the binoculars upward, right into Jake the snake's bedroom. Jake is Wingnut's big brother. He's fourteen years old and he loves snakes.

Jake was there, all right, along with his friends. He stood over the cage of his pet python, Alice, and dangled a little white mouse in the air. I don't think the mouse was too happy about it.

Swallowed by a snake. What a way to go.

Just then, something struck me about Wingnut. He usually came home from school with Freddy Fenderbank. They were best friends. They went together like chocolate and milk.

Something funny was going on. And I

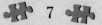 7

don't mean funny ha-ha, or even funny ho-ho. Maybe Freddy and Wingnut had a fight? At least the idea gave me something to think about.

I decided to keep an eye on things.

At exactly 3:10, my brothers Nicholas and Daniel raced into the backyard. They pushed and wrestled each other to be the first one into the tree house. They had been up there a lot lately, ever since Bigs Maloney crushed my ankle.

It wasn't easy to watch.

Sure, I guess the tree house belongs to all of us. But in my heart it was mine, all mine. For half the year, I used that tree house as my detective office. But now, it had been taken over by my brothers.

Worse, I'd seen my sister, Hillary, hanging out in there, too. But never at the same time as Nick and Daniel. Let's just say they don't exactly get along. My brothers had started using the tree house as a launching

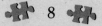

pad for water balloons. Hillary wasn't happy about that.

Just then, there was a knock on my door. It was Grams and Rags, my dog. I figured it must have been Grams who knocked. But with Rags, you never know.

Grams held a deck of cards. She eyed my binoculars.

"Spying on people only leads to trouble, Jigsaw," she said.

"I'd like a bit of trouble, Grams," I confessed. "I'm bored out of my gourd. Besides, I'm a detective. I don't spy. I observe. You never know when a mystery will turn up."

"No," Grams said with a sigh, "I suppose you don't. But if you can tear yourself away from that window for a while, I'll tell you about a mystery that's going on right here in this house."

Chapter Three

The Mystery

Grams sat on my bed and quietly shuffled the deck of cards. Then she dealt seven cards to each of us. Rummy is her game. And she plays to win. When it comes to cards, Grams is all business.

I looked at my hand. It was *crummy*.

"Tell me about this mystery, Grams," I said.

Grams discarded a four of hearts. She picked a new card from the deck.

"My lucky four-leaf clover pin is missing," she said.

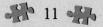

"A missing pin, huh?" I said. I picked up her four and slipped it between a three and a five in my hand, playing for an inside straight. "Like a safety pin?"

"No." She frowned. "A beautiful pin, like the kind a lady wears on her dress or hat."

"Jewelry," I murmured.

Grams picked up a card and tossed down the nine of clubs.

I did my best to focus on the game *and* the case. "Are you sure you didn't drop the pin somewhere?" I asked.

"I never take that pin out of the jewelry box on my dresser," Grams said. "I only wear it one day a year."

"Oh?" I asked.

"St. Patrick's Day," she added. "Which also falls on the day of my wedding anniversary." She paused. "Jigsaw, that's only two days away."

"Well, then this isn't the time to play games," I said. I set down my cards and

grabbed my detective journal. I found a clean page and drew four hearts connected at the points by a stem. (The marker I used was green, for the luck of the Irish. I figured I might need it.)

Beneath the drawing, I wrote:

The Case of the Four-Leaf Clover

"Tell me more about this pin," I said.

Grams smiled and winked at me. Then she laid down her hand. Three sixes and a four-card straight, all hearts.

Maybe I grumbled a little bit. I don't exactly love losing.

Grams told her tale. "Oh, your gramps was a wonderful man," she said. "He had a way of telling the funniest stories. And he always laughed the hardest while he was telling them." She laughed just thinking about it.

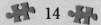

I never got to know Gramps very well. He died a long time ago, when I was little. But somehow, it was like I knew him. I'd heard so many stories and seen so many photos. I knew enough to know that Gramps was somebody special.

"When did he give you the pin, Grams?"

"We had just started keeping company," she said.

"Keeping company?" I asked.

"Dating," she explained.

I made a face and held up a hand. "If this story includes kissing," I pleaded, "then please leave that out."

Grams laughed. "Okay, no smooching. But I did feel like the luckiest girl in the world when I was with your gramps," she said. "We had thirty-six wonderful years together. And one of the ways I remember him is by wearing that pin on St. Patrick's Day."

"I'll find your pin, Grams," I promised. "But you know how it works. I get a dollar a day, no family discounts."

Before we could shake hands on the deal, my sister, Hillary, popped her head in the door. She wore a silk scarf wrapped around her neck.

"Hey, Grams," she called. "Can I borrow this scarf?"

"You can borrow my things anytime, dear," Grams answered. "Just as long as you put them back where you found them."

That was Hillary
for you. She was
always borrowing
stuff from Grams.
Earrings. Handbags.
Hats. Bracelets.

Hmmm . . . pins?

I had a feeling
that the Case of the
Four-Leaf Clover was going to be as easy
as pie.

I wouldn't even have to leave my room.

Chapter Four
Mila

Rags perked up his ears. He lifted his head, barked, and raced downstairs. I figured Mila must be here. Rags was like a furry doorbell . . . that drooled a lot. Every home should have one!

"Sounds like Mila is here for the afternoon shift," Grams said. She slowly lifted herself from the bed. "Never get old, Jigsaw," she advised. "Everything hurts."

When Grams left, I scooted back to the window. Nicholas and Daniel had

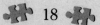 18

rigged a tire swing to one of the branches of the tree right outside. They were taking turns swinging on it.

It looked like fun. Those dirty rats.

"Hey, Worm! Watch this!" Daniel shouted up to my open window. He swung back and forth on the tire a couple of times, climbing higher and higher, and then leaped into the sky. He landed, tumbled, and sprawled in the grass.

"Bet you can't do that!" Nick called to me. Then he added, "Oh, wait. I almost forgot. With that ankle of yours, you can't even walk!"

Then they both roared like it was the funniest joke in the world.

Oh, brother.

Sometimes I hate being the youngest in the family. Older brothers can be such a pain.

I heard Mila coming up the stairs. She

is my best friend and my detective partner. We had solved a lot of mysteries together, from missing hamsters to stinky science projects.

Mila is always singing. She likes to change the words around. Today, she was singing to the tune of "Rain, Rain, Go Away" as she came up the stairs. Only this time she added a twist to it:

"Sprain, sprain, go away.
Don't come again another day.
Jigsaw wants to run and play."

"Hey, Jigsaw," Mila said. She dropped her backpack on the floor and tossed me an ice pack. "I'm here with your homework assignment."

Mila pulled out a note from my teacher, Ms. Gleason, and handed it to me.

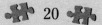

DEAR JIGSAW,

I HOPE YOU ARE FEELING BETTER. WE ALL MISS YOU AND HOPE TO SEE YOU BACK IN CLASS SOON.

PLEASE FINISH THE FOLLOWING WORK FOR NEXT WEEK.

TAKE CARE,
MS. GLEASON

1. MATH:
   COMPLETE THE EXERCISES
   ON PAGES 51-53 OF YOUR
   WORKBOOK.
2. LANGUAGE ARTS:
   WRITE ONE LIMERICK. (ASK MILA
   IF YOU NEED HELP!)

I stopped reading. "A limerick? What's that?"

"It's a poem," Mila said. "It's supposed to be funny, and it rhymes. A, A, B, B, A."

I stared blankly at Mila. What was she trying to spell?

"It's how the rhyme works," Mila explained, smiling. "The last word in lines one, two, and five rhyme with one another. Lines three and four also rhyme. A, A, B, B, A."

"Okaaaaay," I said doubtfully.

"Here, I'll give you an example," Mila offered.

She pulled a large book out of her backpack.

"Ms. Gleason taught us a bunch of limericks by an English writer named Edward Lear. In 1846, he wrote this book, *A Book of Nonsense*. I took it out of the library for you," she said. "I thought you might have some extra time for reading."

I didn't think I'd have *that* much time for reading, and I told Mila so. The book was just slightly smaller than a baby rhino.

"Oh, here's a good one," Mila said. "I'll clap out the rhythm like we did in class.

"There was an old man in a tree
Who was horribly bored by a bee.
When they said, 'Does it buzz?'
He replied, 'Yes, it does!
It's a regular brute of a bee!'"

I might have cracked a smile.

"Here's another!" Mila said, grinning. "I

found this one on the Internet. Its author is anonymous.

"There was an old man of Peru
Who dreamt he was eating his shoe.
He woke in the night
With a terrible fright
And found it was perfectly true!"

This time I laughed out loud.

I didn't think that I could write a limerick that good. But I'd give it a shot. Hey, it's not like I had anything else to do!

Chapter Five

Suspect Number One

Writing a limerick was harder than I thought it would be. I looked at Ms. Gleason's list of tips.

I. PRACTICE THE RHYTHM OF LIMERICKS BY CLAPPING YOUR HANDS OR SNAPPING YOUR FINGERS.

Mila and I did that. But the clapping was sort of weird, and I don't think it helped much.

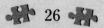

2. THINK OF A FUNNY NAME, PLACE, OR SITUATION.

I looked around the room. Rags was funny. Maybe I could write a poem about my drooling dog. After all, there aren't nearly enough poems about dog slobber.

3. ONCE YOU CHOOSE A SUBJECT, MAKE A LIST OF WORDS THAT RHYME WITH IT.

I jotted down a quick list:

Rags: bags, nags, sags, wags, gags, zigzags, drags

Then I wrote:

I know a dog named Rags,
With a tongue that always sags . . .

I crumpled up the paper and tossed it into my official New York Mets garbage can.

Swish! I spun around in my chair, arms raised in triumph. Rags opened his eyes, blinked twice, and went back to sleep.

"Time for a break?" Mila asked. "I want to hear about our new case."

So I told her about Grams and the missing pin. "I figure that Hillary is

our number one suspect. She probably borrowed the pin and didn't return it."

Mila twisted a strand of long black hair around her finger. "Don't you think Grams would have already thought of that?"

I shrugged and stifled a yawn. "Anyway, we'll need proof," I said. "Got any ideas?"

That instant, Hillary barged into my room. She was making a habit of it.

"Hey, Grams," Hillary called. "Can I borrow your — oh, hey, Worm. Where did Grams go?"

"Didn't you ever hear of knocking?" I complained.

Hillary grinned. "Yeah, I heard of it. So, where's Grams?"

"Not here," I replied.

"Oh, well. Never mind!"

"Hillary, wait!" I called. I zoomed across the room in my rolling chair. It was a nice way to travel.

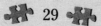

"Mila and I are working on a case," I told my teenage sister. "I have a couple of questions for you."

"Oh, really?" Hillary answered. She pulled off my hat and rumpled my hair. "Well, I'm working on something, too. Gotta run!"

She was out the door and down the stairs before I could say another word.

Suspicious. Very suspicious.

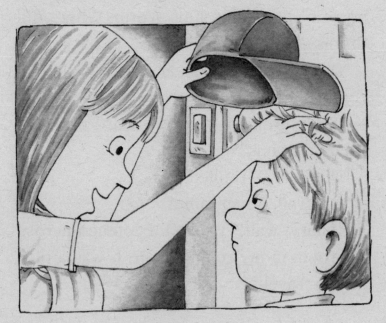

I gave Mila a meaningful look. "See that?" I asked. "She's obviously hiding something."

Mila crossed her arms and rocked back and forth. That's how she gets her thinking machine started.

I glanced out the window to see Hillary crossing the yard toward the tree house. She carried a velvet purse and an old-fashioned hat.

Something strange was going on. If Hillary wouldn't answer our questions, we'd have to try another tactic.

"Mila," I announced. "You're going to have to search my sister's room."

Chapter Six
The Search

"Me?" Mila protested. "I'm not the searching rooms type, Jigsaw. That's your department."

I pointed at my bum foot. "I'll go with you on my crutches, to keep watch. I'll give a signal if Hillary comes back inside."

"A signal?" Mila asked. "What kind of signal?"

I shrugged. "I don't know. I'll probably say something clever like, 'Hillary is coming back inside!'"

Mila thought that was pretty funny.

She looked left down the hallway. She looked right. The coast was clear.

It felt good to finally be doing something. Even if I wasn't the guy doing it.

Mila crept into Hillary's room, and I hobbled behind her. "It's so clean," she said, wrinkling her nose in disapproval.

"My mom made her clean it last night," I explained, squeezing through the doorway

on my crutches. "Usually it looks like it got hit by a tornado."

Mila headed straight for the closet and opened the door. A mountain of stuff fell out—right on top of us!

Guess I knew where Hillary put everything when she cleaned up.

I helped Mila shove everything back in the closet. Then I turned to Hillary's window and looked out at the tree house.

Something strange was going on. Nick was dragging a battered suitcase from the house. From the looks of it, the suitcase was awfully heavy. I wondered what could be inside.

Nick tied a rope to the handle. From his place in the tree house, Daniel hoisted it up.

They smiled at each other, like cats outside a canary cage.

I smelled trouble.

The strangest part was that Hillary seemed to be . . . helping them! She kept looking toward the kitchen window, saying, "Hurry, hurry."

Why would Hillary want to help my rotten, good-for-nothing brothers? All they ever did was give her a hard time.

I glanced over at Mila. "Find anything?" I asked.

"There's no pin in Hillary's jewelry box," Mila whispered. "I'm striking out, Jigsaw. I don't see anything here that belongs to Grams."

I looked back at the tree house. Now Hillary and Nick had scrambled up the ladder. All three of them were in the tree house together, like peas in a pod.

"Check this out, Mila," I said.

She joined me to watch Hillary tack a sheet in front of the tree house window. We could only see the outline of their shadows now.

Listening closely, I heard banging. I heard giggles and laughter. I heard . . . snoring? I looked over my shoulder. It was only Rags.

"Look, Jigsaw. Flashes of light," Mila pointed out.

What in the world were my brothers doing?

And why was Hillary — usually their sworn enemy — working with them?

"Okay, Jigsaw," Mila finally said. "Let's start from the beginning. Tell me everything you've seen through the window. And then tell me what you think it means."

Chapter Seven
A Surprise Visitor

The next morning, my mom came in with my breakfast on a tray: A glass of grape juice, jelly toast, and a bowl of Honey Nut Cheerios.

"The service is pretty good in this place," I joked. Mom fluffed a couple of pillows as I sat up to eat.

"Listen, Jigsaw," she said. "Your father and I are taking Grams shopping this afternoon. Billy is off doing who knows what. So I'm leaving Hillary in charge."

"Isn't that like putting a monkey in charge of the zoo?" I wondered out loud.

"Don't give her a hard time," my mother said, smiling. She propped up my bad ankle and wrapped it in a towel with an ice pack inside. "I'll be back in a few minutes," she said. "Try not to move." And then she was gone. Once again, I was alone in my room.

I could hear the happy chatter of voices from downstairs. If my ankle didn't hurt so much, I would have hopped down there on one leg to join them.

My dad came in to visit a few minutes later. As usual, he had a cup of coffee in one hand.

"We missed you at breakfast this morning, kiddo," he said. "How's the ankle doing?"

"It itches," I complained.

He handed me a piece of paper. It had my name on it. "I found this in the mailbox," he explained. The paper had been folded into a triangle. It was a message from Mila!

I waited until he left. Then I unfolded Mila's note. It was written in code. You can never be too careful. There are spies everywhere!

I HAVE A SURPRISE FOR YOU AFTER SCHOOL.

BE NICE TO HIM!

I recognized the code instantly. I held the paper up to the mirror over my dresser. But even though I could read the words, I still wasn't sure what they meant.

I HAVE A SURPRISE FOR YOU AFTER SCHOOL.
BE NICE TO HIM!

Be nice to *who*? Nick? Daniel? Rags? The question bugged me all day, like a swarm of gnats dive-bombing my head.

As it turned out, the surprise wasn't about the case at all. Mila came over that afternoon. And she brought Bigs Maloney with her. Bigs Maloney, the ankle crusher! The guy who put me in this mess in the first place!

Sure, I knew it was an accident. I knew that Bigs didn't mean to hurt me. But I can't say I was happy to see him. And neither was my ankle. It throbbed *un*happily.

"I'll leave you two alone," Mila said.

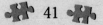

"Wait —" I pleaded. But she was already gone.

Bigs didn't say anything. He just shoved his hands into his pockets and stood there. He stared at his shoelaces, looking uncomfortable.

The thing is, Bigs Maloney is the roughest, toughest kid in the second grade. But I wasn't afraid of him. I knew that Bigs wouldn't hurt a fly. Not on purpose, anyway. Even so, it was his fault I was stuck at home, and we both knew it.

I moaned softly to make him feel worse.

Bigs took a step toward my chair. He reached out his giant hand, dropped it on my shoulder, and squeezed.

I winced. Bigs was about as gentle as a mountain gorilla. He mumbled something that sounded an awful lot like "Urmsury."

I was confused. *Urmsury?* Was that some kind of new language?

Bigs chewed on his lower lip. He dug a

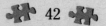

finger into his ear. Finally, he pulled an action figure out of his pocket. It was missing an arm. "Here," Bigs said.

He wanted me to take it, and I didn't argue.

"The arm is kind of busted up. I got mad and sort of ripped it out one day," Bigs told me. "But if you press this button on his back, his eyes light up. Laser vision," he explained. The big lug shifted from one foot to the other. "I want you to have it."

He turned awkwardly toward the door, like he couldn't wait to get away.

But then Bigs stopped and returned to where I sat. He suddenly lurched toward me and wrapped his huge arms around my body.

I felt like I was getting hugged by King Kong.

"Erp," I squeaked.

Whack! Oomph! Bigs clapped me on the back, hard. Either that, or somebody

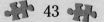

dropped a piano on my head. I wasn't sure which.

Then Bigs marched out the door. He didn't look back. The big guy had made his peace. He came with an apology and a gift. The minute it was over, he left.

I had to hand it to him. The guy had class.

Chapter Eight
Beats TV!

"What did I miss?" Mila asked as she skipped into the room later that afternoon.

"Nothing much," I said. "Bigs squeezed me like a chew toy and whacked me on the back with a sledgehammer."

"I meant in the tree house," Mila said, grinning. She dragged a chair beside me and plopped down into it.

"Hillary has been up in the tree house for about half an hour," I told Mila. "Daniel

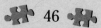

and Nick have been in their bedroom. It's awfully quiet in there. I don't like it."

"Hmmm . . ." Mila said. "Fishy." Then she pulled a bag of popcorn out of her backpack. "This sure beats TV!"

I took a handful of popcorn and stuffed it into my mouth.

"What's Sally Ann been doing?" Mila asked, peering out the window.

"Same old routine," I answered.

"And Wingnut?" she asked.

"He's playing with his hamster again," I replied. Wingnut had built a big maze for Hermie on the floor of his room, and it looked like his friend Freddy had accidentally knocked it over!

Mila pointed at my digital camera. "Hey, pass me that, will you, Jigsaw?" She used the zoom on my camera to take a closer look into Wingnut's room.

"Maybe we should spend less time

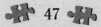 47

spying on people and more time looking for Grams's pin," I said. "After all, great detectives don't solve mysteries by sitting around."

"You're right," Mila said, walking toward the door. "It's time we brought your brothers in for questioning."

"Good idea," I agreed.

Two minutes later, Mila came back with Nicholas and Daniel. I caught her eye, and she pointed at Daniel's right hand. It was covered with marker smudges. A clue!

Nick carried a metal bucket. He set it down near the door.

"What's up, Worm?" Daniel asked. "We have things to do." The boys smiled at each other and snickered.

Daniel pulled a comic book off the shelf and flipped through it. Nick sorted through a stack of my Topps baseball cards.

Mila cleared her throat. "We know you

guys are up to something in the tree house. What is it?"

Nick eyed Daniel and grinned. "We can't tell," he said.

"Yeah, you might get bad dreams," Daniel chimed in.

Nick thought that was pretty funny.

Somehow I forgot to laugh.

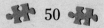

"Where is Grams's pin?" I blurted out.

"Pin?" Nick echoed. "What pin?"

"A green four-leaf clover," I said. "It's missing, and Grams wants it back."

"I have no idea what you're talking about," Nick replied.

Daniel picked up a roll of adhesive tape off my desk. "Can we borrow this?" he asked.

"Not unless you tell me what happened to the pin," I replied.

Nick's eyes narrowed. "Look, Jigsaw. You keep your nose out of our business, you understand?"

"Yeah, stay out of it — or you'll be sorry," Daniel warned.

"*Painfully* sorry," Nick added.

Oh, brother.

"Then we're done here," Mila said, breaking the silence. "Thanks for your time."

Nick and Daniel looked at each other.

They seemed satisfied. Nick picked up the bucket. Daniel tossed the tape into the air and caught it. "Thanks for the tape, Worm."

"Buh-bye!" Nick called cheerfully. The two of them hurried out the door.

Mila rolled her eyes. "Those guys can be sooo annoying," she noted.

"Tell me about it," I muttered.

"They're definitely up to something," she said.

"Yeah, but what?" I wondered.

"Maybe we shouldn't try to find out," Mila said.

"I'm not afraid of them," I told her. Grams needs our help. I'm not going to let Nick and Daniel scare me off."

Chapter Nine

A Plan

"Maybe they're playing a practical joke on Grams?" Mila guessed.

Nick and Daniel have a history of practical jokes. The bucket Nick was carrying had reminded me of a shower I took on April Fools' Day one year — with my clothes on. But I didn't think they'd pull that prank on Grams. When it came to pranks, Grams didn't get mad. She got even.

Mila and I decided to make a list. After all, a mystery is like a jigsaw puzzle. First you have to lay out all the pieces.

Mila wrote out the list:

1. Nick, Daniel, and Hillary are getting along. NOT NORMAL!!!
2. Hillary borrowed a lot of stuff from Grams, but none of it was in her room.
3. Hillary brought an old purse and hat into the tree house.
4. Friday is St. Patrick's Day.
5. Daniel borrowed adhesive tape.
6. There were weird flashes of light in the tree house.
7. The boys lugged a suitcase into the tree house. Something heavy was inside.
8. They didn't want anyone to see what they were doing.

There were a lot of clues. But the pieces just weren't fitting together!

"Don't forget to add the marker smudges on Daniel's hands." I remembered. "That's another clue."

Suddenly, there was a howling outside. At first, I thought it was Rags. But then I realized it was a girl's voice. I turned to the window. Hillary stood at the bottom of the tree, looking up at the tree house.

She was soaking wet.

Nicholas and Daniel leaned out the window with an empty bucket in their hands. They laughed and gave each other a high five.

Hillary clenched her fists. "You guys are impossible!" she shouted. The door slammed behind her — *WHAM!* — as she stormed into the house.

Clomp! Clomp! Clomp! We heard her angry footsteps as she stomped up the stairs.

I reached for a handful of popcorn.

This was getting good.

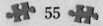 55

Then I looked back out the window. "We have to get a look in the tree house," I murmured.

"We?" Mila said.

"I can use my crutches," I said. "I can —"

"No, Jigsaw," Mila said, "you can't. You need to rest your ankle. So you can go to school next week, play baseball . . ."

". . . and solve mysteries," I added. "I've

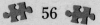

been trying to solve this case while I'm cooped up in my bedroom. And you know where it's gotten me? Nowhere. A big fat zero. Great detectives don't sit around eating popcorn."

"But you can't *walk*," Mila said.

"I have to," I said.

Mila rolled her eyes. "Let's face it, Jigsaw. You are stuck right here, staring out that window." She paused for a moment. "I'll go."

"You heard my brothers," I warned. "They'll be mad if they catch you."

Mila put on a brave face. She grinned, eyes twinkling. "Then I won't let them catch me."

Chapter Ten

Mila, Alone

We had to wait for our chance. And when it came, we were ready.

It happened quickly. I was lounging on the floor, doing a jigsaw puzzle. It was one of those impossible city scenes — all tall buildings and windows. A real brain-buster.

Mila clucked her tongue. She was seated by the window, watching the tree house. "Check this out," she said.

I pulled myself up and sat beside her.

Inside the tree house, Daniel held the

sheet aside. He looked toward our house. Mila and I leaned away from the window. Hopefully, he didn't see us!

Behind Daniel, I glimpsed Nick quickly packing the suitcase.

Then the blanket fell back over the tree house window. Mila and I stayed silent. It was like we were inside a movie. The big action scene was coming soon.

"Come on, guys," I muttered at my brothers. "Don't you ever get hungry? Get out of there, so Mila can take a look inside."

Just then, Nick pulled the sheet off the window. He and Daniel used the rope to lower the suitcase to the ground. They climbed down and, together, dragged the suitcase toward the house.

"This is our chance," Mila whispered. She rose from her chair.

"You don't have to do this," I said. "My

brothers could be back outside at any minute."

Mila shook her head. Her mind was made up. There was no changing it now. "St. Patrick's Day is tomorrow, Jigsaw," she said. "You know how important that pin is to Grams. I'm going."

"Thanks," I said.

And with that, Mila was out the door.

I picked up my binoculars and watched. According to our plan, Mila went out the front door, loudly calling good-bye. Then she snuck around the side of the house to the backyard.

Rags was out there, curled up in the grass. He raised his head, ears perked, eyes curious, to look at Mila.

"Woof," he barked softly. Rags got on all fours. I could tell that he was about to let out a full-blast howl and series of barks.

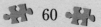

Quickly, Mila offered Rags a pretzel from her pocket. That kept him quiet. Rags is easy that way. He'll do anything for food.

"Come on, Mila," I whispered to myself. "Hurry up."

Mila looked up at my bedroom window. Her head swiveled sharply, looking toward the back door. Had she heard something? Were my brothers coming?

I had to think fast.

"HEY, GUYS!" I screamed. "NICK! DANIEL! COME UP HERE, QUICK!"

I looked out the window, waving frantically. "Now," I mouthed. "This is your chance."

I heard the clatter of footsteps on the stairs.

As if reading my mind, Mila moved swiftly to the tree house ladder. In a moment, she was up.

My door burst open.

"What do you want?" Daniel asked.

"I'm done with my popcorn. Could you bring the bowl downstairs for me?" I asked.

Nick grabbed the empty bowl. "You're a real pain, you know that?"

I smiled. They had no idea.

Chapter Eleven
Trapped!

As soon as my brothers left, I turned back to the window. *"Hurry up, Mila,"* I muttered.

She looked out the tree house window and raised her hands. She wasn't finding anything.

My eyes scanned the yard. There was no sign of my brothers. I thought I heard the refrigerator open down in the kitchen. Good. Those guys could eat all day, once they got started.

I noticed that Mila bent down. Then she looked out the window at me. A wide smile crossed her face. She held up a closed fist in triumph.

Click . . .

That's when I heard it. The back door opening and banging closed.

Nick and Daniel were outside again.

Mila ducked right away. I saw that Nick held a Frisbee. Maybe they weren't going to the tree house, after all. Maybe they were just going to have a quick toss. Maybe they would even walk over to Lincoln Park.

And maybe hippos flew in purple helicopters.

Nick led the way to the tree house ladder.

Mila was trapped! There was nowhere for her to hide.

I tried to imagine what Nick and Daniel would do if they caught *me* snooping around in their stuff. Tickle torture? Or maybe they would pin me down, sit on my chest, and threaten to drool on my face?

 65

They were capable of all sorts of things. They are, after all, older brothers. It's what they do.

But . . . they wouldn't do any of those things to Mila, right? It's not like she's their sister or anything. Though, in a way, Mila is like family. Some days, she practically lives at our house.

I gulped.

She was dead meat.

And there was nothing I could do about it.

Nick and Daniel climbed the ladder quickly. I could see their heads appear in the tree house window.

They were clearly surprised to discover Mila there.

But Mila was smiling and talking. She seemed lighthearted, laughing. The whole time she kept her right hand behind her back. Was she crossing her fingers for luck?

No, Mila was holding something. She knew I was watching. She was trying to show me what she had in her hand. It was green, and it shimmered in the slanting sunlight.

Grams's pin!

The four-leaf clover!

Mila had the pin!

Too bad my brothers had Mila.

I saw Nick cross his arms. Daniel raised an eyebrow. They weren't buying whatever story Mila was selling. She was in deep trouble. I had to do something.

I flung open the window.

I was about to shout something, anything. I didn't know what. But then I saw Mila backing toward the ladder.

They were letting her go!

"Go, Mila," I muttered. I leaned back in my chair. Maybe luck was on our side, after all.

Mila climbed down the ladder. Rags barked, and she patted him on the head.

Then Mila skipped across the yard — light as a feather — and out the gate.

Mila was smart. She couldn't let my brothers see her head back into our house. I followed her with the binoculars, hoping that she'd give me some kind of signal. But that was my big mistake.

I should have been more careful.

Because when I looked back at the tree house, I saw my brothers staring right at me.

And they weren't happy.

My luck had just run out.

Chapter Twelve
Blinded by the Light

My heart pounded. My throat went dry. My ankle throbbed. Nick and Daniel pointed at me. They nodded, grinning like madmen.

They were coming to get me.

I had nowhere to run.

Heck, I had nowhere to even hop.

I pushed myself over to the door and locked it. That wouldn't hold them off for long. Daniel is a master lock-picker. But maybe I could keep them out until my parents got home.

Maybe not.

I heard the back door close. Two sets of footsteps climbed the stairs. The steps were slow and determined. They weren't in a rush at all. Nick and Daniel were going to take their time. After all, they were enjoying this.

Torturing little brothers. What could be more fun?

I heard them draw closer and closer.

I rolled my chair back to the window. For a minute, I wondered if I could climb out.

Maybe my brothers wouldn't hurt Mila. But there was no telling what they'd do to me.

There were three loud, steady knocks on the door. *Knock. Knock. Knock.* The knocks turned into pounding.

Then they tried the doorknob.

"We know you're in there, little brother," Daniel called. His voice sounded like it had been sweetened with honey.

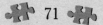 71

"Yeah, and you know we're coming in," promised Nicholas, "one way or the other."

I looked around the room for something, anything, I could use to defend myself. Without really thinking, I grabbed the camera. I turned it on and set it for FLASH. It was all I could come up with. I pulled down the window shade and flicked off the light.

The room went dark.

Should I try to hide under the bed? In the closet?

The doorknob jiggled. And then — *click* — it turned.

I held the camera above my head.

The door swung open. My brothers seemed to hover in the doorway, thrown off by the darkness. A beam of light lit them from behind. They seemed bigger than I remembered. Scarier.

Click! I snapped their picture. The flash went off, blinding them for a minute. They shielded their eyes with their arms. But

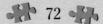 72

my trick didn't stop them. They came closer, step by step.

Click!

Blinded again.

Closer.

"You can't hold us off forever, Worm," said Nicholas.

Another flash.

"Yeah," added Daniel. "This is the end of the road, little brother."

Another flash. *Click!* Then another.

Soon they were at my chair. They grabbed me and rolled me away from the window.

I couldn't run.

This was it.

I was a goner.

Chapter Thirteen
Saved

"Bwahhh-haaa-haaa!" Nicholas laughed. Daniel joined in. Then Nick held my wrists pinned to my sides, and Daniel tickled me under my arms . . . on my sides . . . behind my knees.

"No, stop," I begged. "Not tickle torture! Anything but tickle torture!" My sides ached from laughing so hard. Tears started to roll from my eyes.

That's when Mila burst through the door. "Stop!" she demanded. Rags came

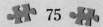

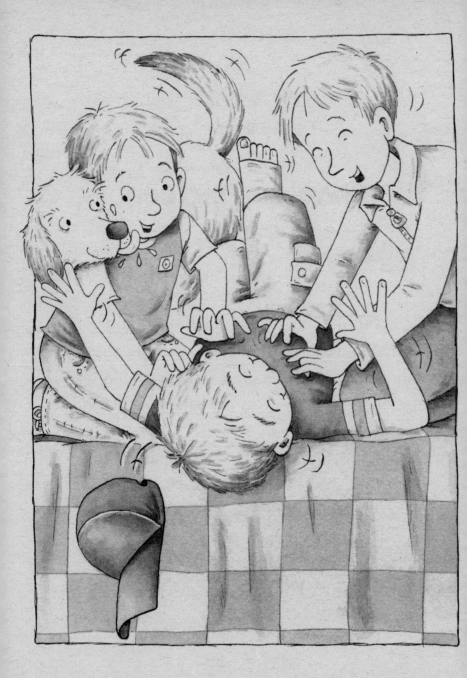

bounding into the room behind her. He jumped up on Nick and Daniel, panting and drooling, licking their faces like it was a happy game. In all the confusion, they let me go.

Thank goodness for Mila . . . and good old Rags.

"Okay, okay," said Daniel. "We surrender! Call off Rags."

Hillary walked in carrying her cell phone and frowning.

"Can you puh-*lease* stop screaming?" she said. "You guys are ridiculous."

I sat up on the bed. Mila tossed me Grams's pin. I tucked it into my pocket for safekeeping.

"I found it in the tree house," Mila explained.

"Okay," I said, my tone sharp. "Who stole the pin? And why?"

Hillary snapped her phone shut. She slumped down on the bed, glaring at my

brothers the whole time. She clearly wasn't happy with them.

"Spill it," I said.

"Nobody *stole* anything," Nick said. "We *borrowed* it."

"Yeah, right," I muttered.

"There's a difference," Daniel protested. "Grams always said that it's okay to borrow her stuff —"

"— as long as you put it back where it belongs," Hillary chimed in. "And you guys didn't return it. That was *your* job. Besides, you didn't even ask to borrow it." She turned to Mila. "I always ask first."

Nick made a singsong noise. Something like, "La-di-da, di-da-da."

Hillary rolled her eyes.

I sensed a fight coming on, so I jumped in.

"That doesn't explain why you borrowed the pin in the first place," I insisted.

"This might explain it," Mila said. "The pin wasn't the only thing I found."

Mila pulled a neatly wrapped package from behind her back.

Nick and Daniel looked at her in astonishment and admiration. "I went back for it after you guys headed into the house," she explained.

The wrapping paper was grass green. It was decorated with a white ribbon, tied in a

 79

bow. I started to get an idea of what was inside.

My mind flashed back to Mila's list of clues. The puzzle pieces began to fit together.

The secrets were really just part of a surprise gift! The clothes borrowed from Grams were memories from the past. The flashes of light from the tree house were photographs being taken. The marker smudges, the tape, it all fit in. And, of course, tomorrow was Grams's special day.

The pieces were in place. I had a clear picture. But I wasn't going to be the one to unwrap the package. Because the gift wasn't for me.

Grams was going to open it.

Maybe, just maybe, my rotten brothers weren't so rotten after all.

Could that be true?

Chapter Fourteen
Solved

"You guys made Grams a scrapbook for her anniversary," Mila said. "That's what's in the package."

"Yes," I said. "That's what you've been working on in the tree house."

"Nice work, Sherlock," Daniel said, smiling. "It sure took you long enough to figure it out."

"We wanted to let you in on it, Jigsaw," Hillary added. "But you've been spending so much time with Grams, we were afraid you'd let the secret slip."

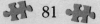 81

"That, and we thought you could use a little mystery in your world. Poor Wormy, trapped in his bedroom all day," Nick said.

"Yeah," Daniel added. "You had to be bored if you were watching us through the window for three days straight."

I felt my cheeks grow red. They had known all along that I was watching them.

"It started out as a simple photo album," Hillary said. "But we couldn't find pictures of everything."

"We decided to re-create some scenes from Grams's life. You know how Hillary loves to act," Nick added, waving his hand for effect. "So we dressed up in costumes and took photos."

That explained the flashes of light in the tree house.

"It was fun," Hillary went on. "I dressed up like Grams. Daniel was Gramps."

"Yeah, fun," Daniel said. "Except for the

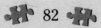

story of how Grams met Gramps. That was a little gross." They all burst out laughing.

I began to feel a little bad. Like I had missed something important. I could see that the three of them had had a good time together.

"So," said Hillary, taking charge, "we carried all the supplies up to the tree house in that old suitcase. We figured Grams would never suspect what was going on out there."

"Yeah," Nick said. "But we didn't realize that the house detective would figure it out so fast — and almost mess up our big surprise."

"Pretty clever, Jigsaw," Daniel said. He looked at Mila. "You, too, Mila. It seems to me like you did all the heavy lifting for this case."

One thing still bugged me.

"Why did you drop the bucket of water

on Hillary's head after you guys had been working together?" I asked.

Nick looked at Daniel, who smirked back. Together, they shrugged and said, "Why not? It seemed like a good idea at the time!"

They burst into loud laughter.

Even Hillary had to laugh after a while.

Some things never change. But outside my window, things were looking different now.

Sally Ann Simms was back outside. She had hung a curtain from a tree branch to make a stage. She twirled around in her tutu as a man in a business suit came out of the back door of her house.

He had the same goofy grin as Sally Ann —
only he had all his front teeth.

Mr. Simms swept Sally Ann up in his arms
and twirled her around. It looked like he had
just gotten home from a business trip. And
Sally Ann had found the perfect audience.

I glanced up at Wingnut's bedroom
window. He was back in
his room with Hermie.
Only this time, Jake the
snake was with
him. They both
looked happier
than I'd seen them
all week.

I guess we were
all feeling a little less
lonely now.

Nick, Daniel, and Hillary gave Grams the
scrapbook the next night, over a traditional
Irish dinner of corned beef and cabbage.
(I prefer pizza, thank you very much.)

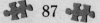

Grams's eyes grew wet and shone in the light. She carefully turned the pages of the book, her fingertips reaching  out to touch the pictures. Some made her laugh. Others, well, they touched her heart in a different way. We could tell it was a good present. And glued to the inside back cover was an extra-special limerick written by *me*. I'd finally gotten the hang of it. I had just needed something great to write about!

Then I gave Grams the pin, wrapped up in a little box. She fastened it to her blouse right away and kept touching it all night.

"Thank you, Jigsaw," she said. "You are a fine detective."

I grinned. "You should see me when I have two good feet!"

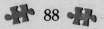

After that, the whole family played cards together. I could tell that Daniel and Nick tried hard not to be too rotten.

Just for one night.

For Grams.

Of course, nobody could beat Grams at cards that night. But we all still felt lucky.

Go figure.

About the Author

James Preller often draws upon his own life as a basis for his Jigsaw Jones books. Like Jigsaw, James Preller has a slobbering, sock-eating dog. Like Jigsaw, James was the youngest in a large family. His older brothers called him Worm and worse — yeesh! And so do Jigsaw's!

James and Jigsaw both love jigsaw puzzles, baseball, grape juice, and mysteries. But even though Jigsaw and James have so much in common, they are not the same person.

Unlike Jigsaw, James Preller is the author of many books for children. He lives in Delmar, New York, with his wife, Lisa, three kids — Nicholas, Gavin, and Maggie — his two cats, and his dog.

Learn more at www.jamespreller.com

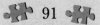

Puzzling Codes
and
Activities

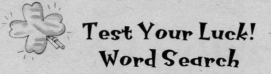

Test Your Luck!
Word Search

Can you find the words hidden below, detective?
Words can be horizontal, vertical, diagonal, and
even backward!

Clover * Green * St. Patrick * Irish * March *
Shamrock * Limerick

A	I	C	L	O	V	E	R	S	G	E	S
B	K	R	H	N	I	L	G	A	R	O	T
W	C	Z	I	E	Q	R	D	E	A	B	P
R	O	K	P	S	E	Y	I	L	S	F	A
L	R	N	U	E	H	M	P	S	D	E	T
H	M	A	N	B	S	A	T	P	L	N	R
F	A	I	O	R	Y	R	D	W	S	P	I
S	H	A	L	M	N	C	V	T	Y	B	C
F	S	J	K	F	R	H	Y	E	M	P	K
L	I	M	E	R	I	C	K	B	N	O	N

Answers on page 103

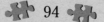

Rhyme Time!

In *The Case of the Four-Leaf Clover*, Jigsaw and Mila learn all about writing limericks (see page 22)! These are funny poems that rhyme using the A, A, B, B, A structure. The last word in the lines one, two, and five rhyme with one another. Lines three and four also rhyme.

Example:

There was an old man in a tree (A)
Who was horribly bored by a bee (A)
When they said, "Does it buzz?" (B)
He replied, "Yes, it does! (B)
It's a regular brute of a bee!" (A)

The (A) words all rhyme: *tree, bee, bee.*
The (B) words both rhyme, too: *buzz, does.*

Now, try writing your own limerick!

_____ (A)

_____ (A)

_____ (B)

_____ (B)

_____ (A)

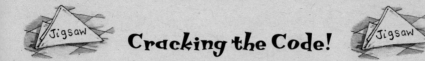

Good detectives use lots of different codes to communicate. You never know who might be reading your notes!

In *The Case of the Four-Leaf Clover*, Mila uses a mirror code to send Jigsaw a message. Can you crack the mirror code below?

GREAT JOB, DETECTIVE!
NICE CODE-CRACKING SKILLS!

Write the answer below:

_____

_____

Answers on page 104.

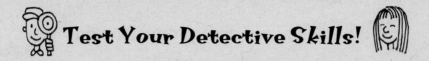

Test Your Detective Skills!

Look carefully at the picture below. Then turn the page and answer the questions as best you can. Can you remember all the details about this picture, detective?

1. What is Jigsaw's foot propped up on?

_____

2. Who is Jigsaw sitting with?

_____

3. What is behind Jigsaw?

_____

4. Does Jigsaw have his hat on forward or backward?

_____

5. Is the person next to Jigsaw wearing pants or a skirt?

_____

Answers on page 104.

 98

From the Top Secret Pages of Jigsaw Jones' Detective Journal

Now you can solve mysteries like Jigsaw Jones and Mila Yeh!

Case: The case of _____

Client: _____

Suspects: _____
_____

Clues: _____
_____

Key Words: _____
_____

Mystery Solved: _____
_____

From the Top Secret Pages of Jigsaw Jones' Detective Journal

Now you can solve mysteries like Jigsaw Jones and Mila Yeh!

Case: The case of _____

Client: _____

Suspects: _____

_____

Clues: _____

_____

Key Words: _____

_____

Mystery Solved: _____

_____

From the Top Secret Pages of Jigsaw Jones' Detective Journal

Now you can solve mysteries like Jigsaw Jones and Mila Yeh!

Case: The case of _____

Client: _____

Suspects: _____
_____

Clues: _____
_____

Key Words: _____
_____

Mystery Solved: _____
_____

From the Top Secret Pages of Jigsaw Jones' Detective Journal

Now you can solve mysteries like Jigsaw Jones and Mila Yeh!

Case: The case of _____

Client: _____

Suspects: _____

_____

Clues: _____

_____

Key Words: _____

_____

Mystery Solved: _____

_____

Answers

Test Your Luck!
Word Search

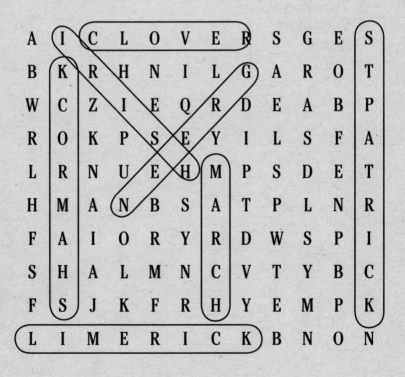

Cracking The Code!

GREAT JOB, DETECTIVE!
NICE CODE-CRACKING SKILLS!

Test Your Detective Skills!

1. A stool
2. Grams
3. Tree house
4. Backward
5. A skirt